For my Family
And all our years down the Shore

This paperback edition published in 2012 by Andersen Press Ltd.
First published in USA in 2006 by Clarion Books,
an imprint of Houghton Mifflin Harcourt Publishing Company.

Published by special arrangement with Clarion Books,
an imprint of Houghton Mifflin Harcourt Publishing Company,
and Rights People, London.

Printed and bound in China.

10   9   8   7

British Library Cataloguing in Publication Data available.

ISBN 978 1 84939 449 9

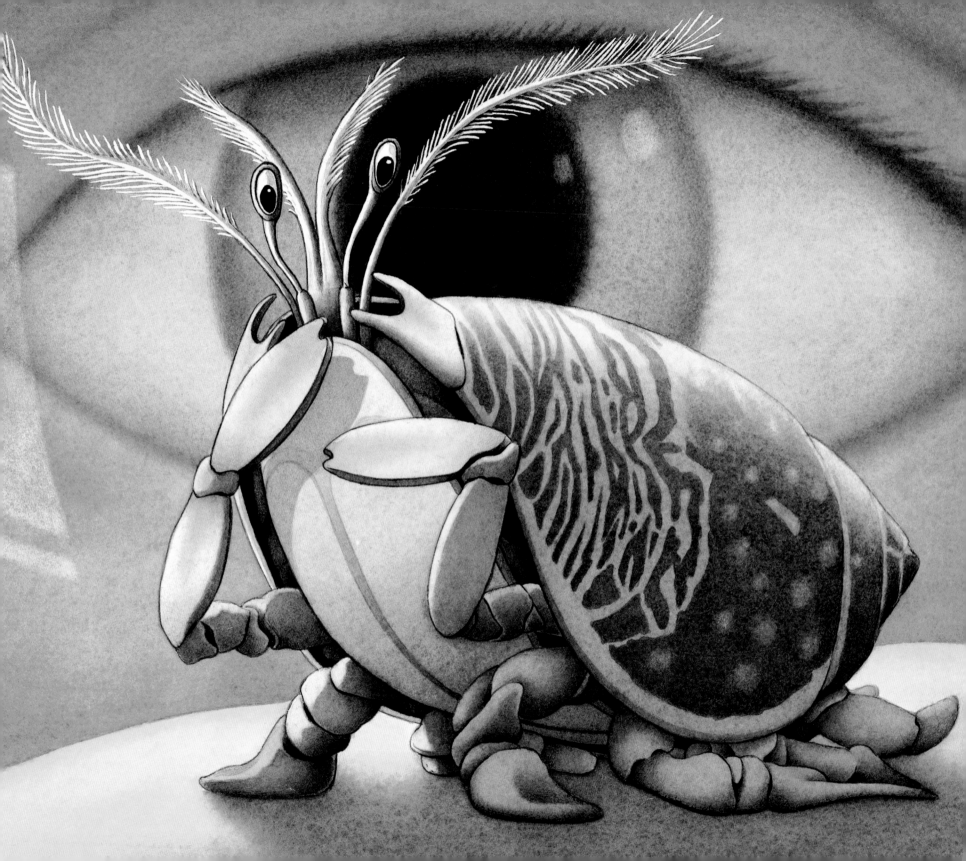

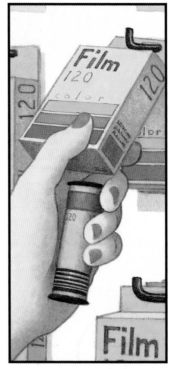

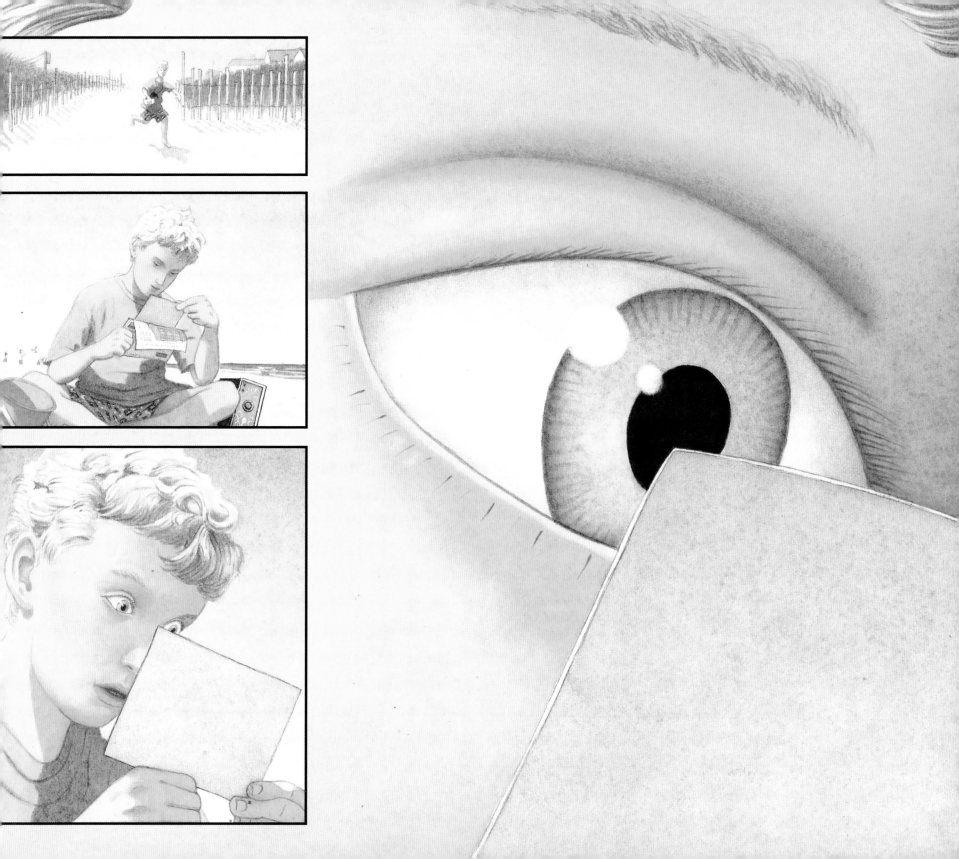

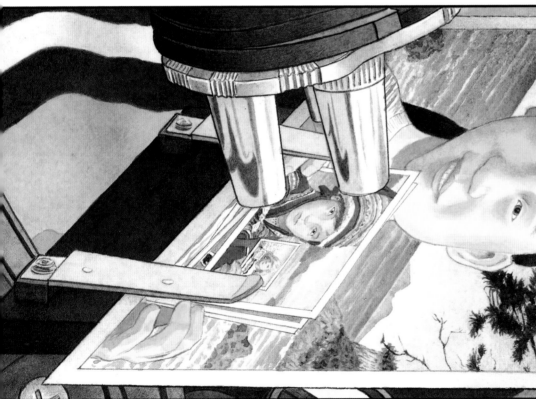

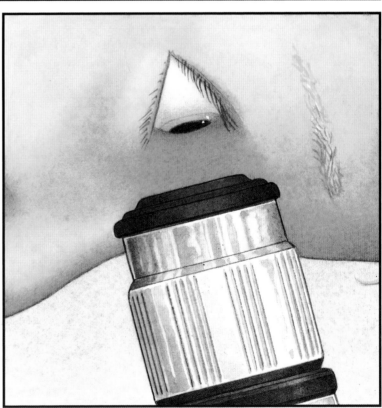

10 x

25 x

40 x

55 x

70 x

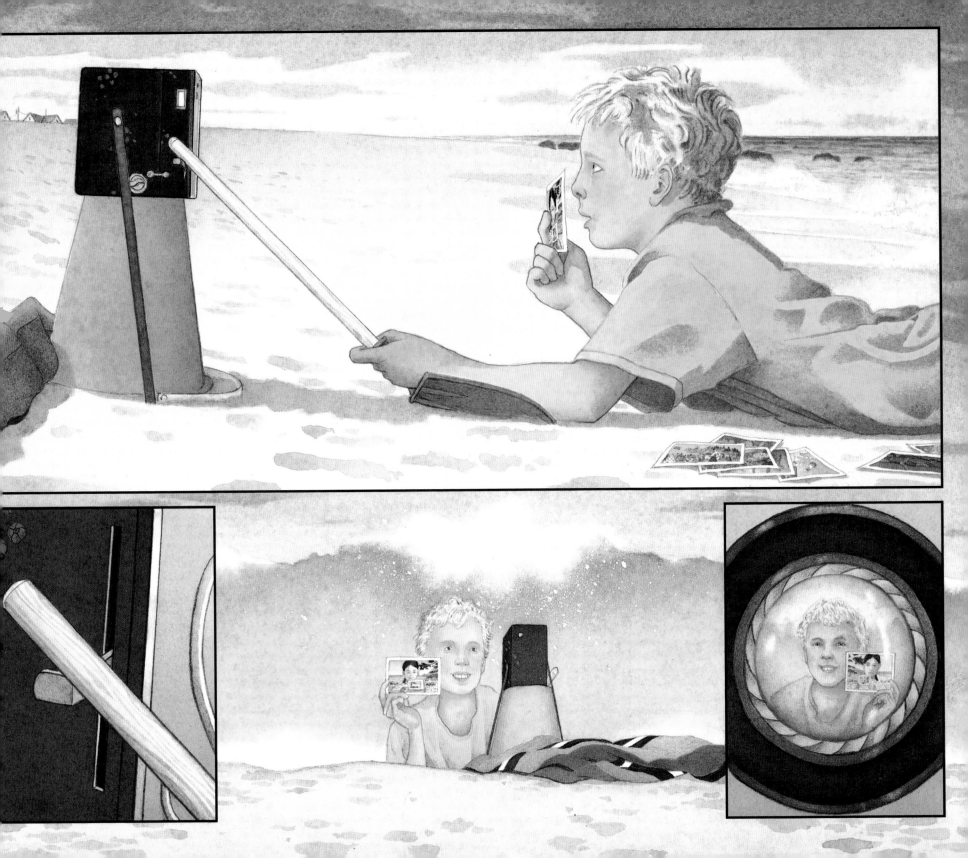

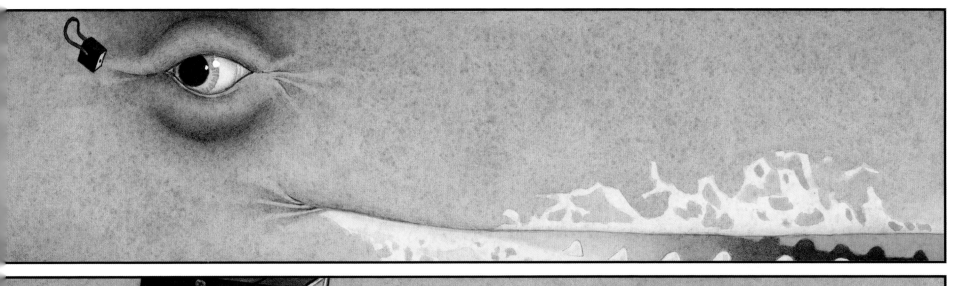

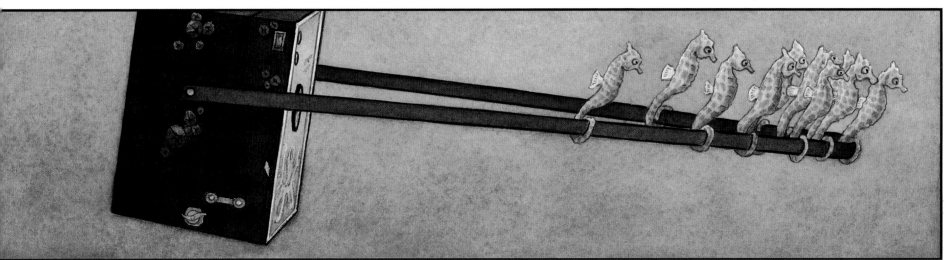